Tyra
the Dress Designer
Fairy

by Daisy Meadows

ORCHARD

www.rainbowmagic.co.uk

The Fairyland Palace

Tippington Fountain SHOPPING CENTRE

Fashion Show

Top hats & tiaras

HARTLEY'S

"Ice Blue" Hair Salon

TIPPINGTON TOYS

"Ice Blue" Stall

Jack Frost's Spell

I'm the king of designer fashion,
Looking stylish is my passion.
Ice Blue's the name of my fashion range,
Some people think my clothes are strange.

Do I care, though? Not a bit!
My designer label will be a hit.
The Fashion Fairies' magic will make that come true:
Soon everyone will wear Ice Blue!

Contents

Funny Fashions

"I can't wait for the Design-and-Make Competition workshop to start," said Kirsty Tate, peering into her bag in excitement. "I've got my colourful scarves and I'm going to sew them into a floaty dress."

"It will be great!" said her best friend Rachel Walker. "I'm going to paint a glittery rainbow on my old jeans."

"And I'm going to have lunch with my friend Moira," said Mrs Walker. "So we all have an enjoyable day in store!"

They were all standing inside the new *Tippington Fountains Shopping Centre.* Kirsty was staying with Rachel for the half-term holiday, and they had been having a very exciting time ever since the shopping centre opened. A Design-and-Make Competition had been announced on the opening day, and the girls had been working on their ideas ever since. After the workshop, their creations would be judged, and the winners would model their clothes in a charity fashion show at the end of the week.

"Let's go this way," said Mrs Walker. "I said that I'd meet Moira outside the wedding dress shop, *Top Hats & Tiaras*."

They walked along slowly, looking at all the exciting new shops on either side. Then Rachel nudged Kirsty. "Look at that lady over there," she said. "She's wearing one long trouser leg and one short."

"Her son only has one sock on," said Kirsty. "That's strange."

"New fashions always seem strange at first," said Mrs

Walker with a laugh. "Look, there's
Moira over there, and she's got safety
pins on her cardigan instead of buttons.
Whatever will the fashion designers think
of next?"

As Mrs Walker went to give Moira a

hug, Kirsty
and Rachel
exchanged a
glance.

"These aren't
funny new
fashions," said
Rachel. "It's
Jack Frost and
his naughty
goblins causing

trouble!"

At the start of the week, Kirsty and

Rachel had gone to see their fairy friends in a fashion show. But Jack Frost and his goblins had barged in, wearing ugly ice-blue outfits. The Ice Lord had created his own designer label called Ice Blue. He wanted everyone in the human world and Fairyland to wear his clothes, so they would all look just like him!

With a bolt of icy magic, Jack had stolen the Fashion Fairies' magical objects and brought them to *Tippington Fountains Shopping Centre*. The fairies needed their magical objects to look after every aspect of fashion in both the human world and in Fairyland. Now everything in the fashion world was going wrong.

"I'll see you at the competition later,"

called Mrs Walker.
"Have fun, girls!"

Kirsty and
Rachel waved
goodbye.

"We've still got
half an hour before
the workshop starts,"
said Rachel. "Let's go and see if we can
find any goblins."

The poor Fashion Fairies had asked
for the girls' help, and of course Kirsty
and Rachel had said yes! They had
already helped two of the fairies to get
their objects back. But Jack Frost and his
goblins were becoming more and more
sly. Would they be able to find the other
objects in time to save the fashion show
at the end of the week?

The girls started their search for goblins in *Hartley's Department Store*.

"Don't forget to look under shelves and behind rails," said Kirsty. "Goblins can hide in really tiny spaces. They could be anywhere."

Rachel started to check a rail of tops, while Kirsty got down on her knees and peered under a low shelf.

"Look at this," said Rachel, holding up a blouse that was full of large holes. "What a fashion disaster!"

Kirsty shook her head sadly, stood up and then tripped over.

"Are you all right?" asked Rachel, hurrying over to help her friend.

"I'm fine," said Kirsty. "But what made me fall over?" They looked down and saw a pair of trousers trailing on the ground from a clothes rail.

"Those trouser legs are much too long," said Rachel. "Oh dear, we have to find the goblins and stop them!"

16

Everywhere the girls looked in the shop, they found clothes that were misshapen, torn or stained. They stopped beside a display of autumn fashions and Kirsty groaned.

"Look at that!" she exclaimed.

The mannequin in the middle of the display had a split up the back of her jeans! The girls looked at the others in the display, checking if their clothes were spoiled. As Rachel examined a mannequin in a long, golden-brown dress, she noticed something strange.

"That dress looks almost as if it's glowing," she said. "Down by the right-hand pocket – can you see it, Kirsty?"

"Yes!" said Kirsty, moving closer. "It looks like…magic!"

A Worrying Workshop

There was a fizz of sparkling fairy dust, and then Tyra the Dress Designer Fairy climbed out of the dress pocket!

"Hello, Tyra!" said the girls in excitement.

Tyra looked cool in her ruffled skirt and funky, leopard-print braces, but her dark eyes were worried.

"Hello, Kirsty!" she replied. "Hello, Rachel. I'm here to try and get my magical tape measure back from Jack Frost and the goblins. Everywhere I go I see awful-looking clothes that don't fit properly, and it's making me really sad that I can't do my job!"

"We've seen some strange fashions too," said Kirsty. "Don't worry, Tyra. We'll help you. We've already been looking for goblins this morning."

"Did you find any?" Tyra asked.

"Not yet," said Rachel. "Let's keep searching."

"But we have to go to the workshop," said Kirsty, looking at her watch. "It's about to start!"

"What about Tyra?" asked Rachel.

"No problem," said Tyra, zooming into

Kirsty's bag of scarves. "I'll hide in here. Fabulous colours, Kirsty!"

The girls hurried to the magnificent fountain area in the middle of the shopping centre. It was crowded with girls and boys, who were all sitting at long tables. The tables were piled high with ribbons, sequins and colourful material in lots of different textures and sizes.

"Look, there's Jessica Jarvis!" said Rachel, noticing the supermodel who was helping to organise the competition.

"And there's Ella McCauley," Kirsty added, spotting the famous dress designer.

The two celebrities were setting up the last table for the workshop. As Rachel and Kirsty moved towards two empty chairs, they saw Ella look down at her arms in surprise.

"Oh my goodness, this top has one sleeve longer than the other!" she exclaimed. "How could I have missed that? How embarrassing!"

"No one will notice if you roll them both up,"

said Jessica. "Look at what I've done
– I'm wearing two different-coloured
shoes!"

Rachel and Kirsty took their places
at one of the tables with all the other
girls and boys. Everyone was chattering
eagerly, and no one seemed to have
noticed the strange fashion mistakes that
the celebrities had made.

"I can't see any goblins lurking
around," said Rachel in a low voice.
"I hope that they stay away from the
workshop!"

Tyra peeped over the top of Kirsty's
bag.

"I'm worried about the workshop," she
said, frowning. "If Jessica and Ella are
having fashion disasters, anything could
happen!"

At that moment, Ella clapped her hands together and the chattering girls and boys fell silent.

"Hi, everyone," said Ella. "It's great that so many of you have turned up for the workshop. Some of you already know that I'm a dress designer, and that makes me very lucky. I get to do something that I love every day!"

Her eyes were sparkling with interest and excitement. Rachel noticed that she had rolled up her sleeves.

"When I'm designing a new dress, I start by drawing it on paper," Ella went on. "Then I choose the fabric I want to use, and measure it up carefully. Finally I sew the pieces together to make the dress."

It sounded wonderful, and Kirsty felt as if her fingers were itching to get started.

"I'd like you all to meet Mabel," said Ella.

She brought out a life-size dressmaker's mannequin, which was coloured purple. There was a dial on Mabel's back that looked a bit like a watch face. There were numbers printed around the edge.

"By turning this dial, I can change Mabel's dress size," Ella continued. "It means that I can design clothes for people of all different shapes and sizes."

Ella handed round some of her designs so that everyone could see how to start designing.

"You can find paper and pencils on the tables," she announced. "Start planning your designs, and I will walk around and help anyone who needs advice."

Kirsty and Rachel picked up their pencils and started to sketch. They had imagined their outfits so many times that it was easy to draw every detail.

"I love your floaty dress," said Rachel, looking at Kirsty's drawing.

"I'd buy your jeans if I saw them in a shop," Kirsty replied with a grin.

"Me too," said a voice behind them.

They looked around and saw Ella looking over their shoulders. She smiled at them.

"I think both your designs are fantastic," she said. "Let me help you to measure up the scarves and jeans you're using." She took out a tape measure and

stretched it along Rachel's jeans. Then she took out a small white pencil.

"This is a dressmaking pencil," she said. "I use it to mark measurements on clothes without damaging them."

She leaned forward and then paused.

"I don't believe it!" she exclaimed.

Goblins in Blue

"Look at the numbers on this tape measure," said Ella. "They're all muddled up!"

Rachel and Kirsty looked down. Sure enough, all the numbers were in the wrong order.

"This is because Tyra's magic tape measure is missing," whispered Kirsty.

"What are we going to do without a tape measure?" asked Rachel, feeling worried that she wouldn't be able to finish her design.

"Don't panic," said Ella. "I have a few tricks up my sleeve!" She winked at them and pulled a ball of string out of her pocket.

"You can mark the measurements using a length of string," she said. "It'll work just as well."

As Ella moved away, Tyra looked up at the girls.

"I'm going to go and see if I can spot the goblins while you finish your clothes," she said. "There's a beautiful flower basket hanging  from the railings on the first floor, and it overlooks the fountain area. I'll be able to see any goblins from up there – and keep an eye on you too!"

The girls started making their outfits, while Tyra fluttered up to the flower basket, making sure that no one saw her.

Rachel concentrated on drawing the rainbow on her jeans with glittery paint, while Kirsty started to sew her scarves together.

After a few minutes, the girls heard a groan from the table next to them. They saw a boy holding up a shirt that was several sizes too big. Rachel looked down at her jeans.

"Oh no!" she exclaimed. "Look, Kirsty – my rainbow stripes are all wobbly."

Kirsty put her
arm around
her friend's
shoulders.

"I'll help
you fix
them," she
said in a
comforting
voice. "I'll just go
and try on my scarf-
dress, and then we can repaint the stripes
together."

She carefully picked up her dress and
took it to the curtained-off fitting room
in the corner. A few moments later she
came out, swishing the dress around and
smiling.

"That looks wonderful!" cried Rachel.

Kirsty stood in front of the mirror and looked carefully at her creation. Then her smile faded.

"The hem is lopsided!" she groaned. "Look, Rachel – it's longer on the left than on the right. And I thought I measured it so carefully!"

Kirsty changed back into her ordinary clothes. When she came out of the fitting room, Rachel beckoned to her and put her finger to her lips.

"Can you hear something?" she whispered.

Kirsty strained her ears. Over the chatter of the other girls and boys, she could hear a faint voice like the far-off tinkling of bells.

"Kirsty! Rachel!"

"It's Tyra!" said the girls together.

They looked up and saw Tyra leaning out of the flower basket, beckoning to them. She had her wand pressed to her throat.

"She must be using magic so that we can hear her," said Kirsty.

"She's pointing at something over there," Rachel cried. "What has she seen?"

Tyra was pointing to a group of four boys arriving at one of the workshop tables. They were all wearing bright-blue outfits with zany, high shoulders and tight trousers.

"Look at their enormous shoes!" said Kirsty. "They're goblins, I'm sure of it!"

"That must be why Tyra was pointing at them," Rachel agreed. "Come on, let's get closer. We have to find out what they're up to!"

The goblins' table was piled high with fabric in many different shades of blue. Beside it was a dressmaker's mannequin on wheels. But it was nothing like Mabel. This mannequin was tall and blue. When one of the goblins spun it around, Kirsty gasped. It looked exactly like Jack Frost!

Suddenly, Kirsty felt

something gauzy tickle the back of her neck. Tyra had flown down and tucked herself under a lock of Kirsty's hair.

"Can you and Rachel go somewhere private?" said Tyra quietly. "I think we'll have a better chance of finding the magic tape measure if I transform you into fairies."

Kirsty touched Rachel's arm.

"Tyra wants to turn us into fairies," she said in a low voice. "Let's hide in the fitting room."

They told Ella that they were going to fetch something that would help them with their designs, and then hurried into the dim changing room. Tyra fluttered out and waved her wand over the girls, making their skin tingle. A puff of rainbow-coloured fairy dust billowed

around them, and
gossamer wings
unfurled from
their shoulders
as they shrank
to fairy-size.

The three
fairies fluttered
out of the fitting
room and made
their way towards
the goblins' table. They flitted between
baskets of material, being very careful to
stay out of sight.

"Let's hide in here," said Rachel,
slipping under a large pile of blue fabric.
"Now we'll be able to hear everything
the goblins say."

Shopping Centre Chaos

The goblins were chattering and squawking, and sounded very pleased with themselves.

"Does anyone need any help?" asked Jessica, who was just walking past the table.

"Not from you!" said the rude goblins.

Jessica looked surprised, but walked away.

"Jack Frost is going to love this outfit," said a short goblin with a long nose. "He's bound to reward us for this."

"I think he'll like my bit best," said another goblin, who had a blue scarf wrapped around his waist like a belt.

"No chance," sneered a third goblin, who had a blue top hat balanced on his bony head. "Mine's better than yours."

"Each of them is making a different section of the outfit," Kirsty realised. "Look – that goblin's got the collar, and this one has a trouser leg."

"What a funny way to make an outfit," said Tyra, frowning.

"Give me that tape measure," demanded a skinny goblin with a pimple on the tip of his nose.

"What's the magic word?" demanded the goblin with the scarf.

"NOW!" squawked the skinny goblin.

There was a little tussle and then the skinny goblin grabbed a shiny golden tape measure from the other's hand. Tyra gasped.

"That's my magic tape measure!" she said, clasping Rachel's hand in excitement. "We've found it!"

"No wonder the goblins are finding it easy to make the outfit," said Kirsty. "They've got your magic to help them, Tyra!"

"That's it!" announced the skinny goblin. "I've finished. Let's put the outfit together."

The goblins scrambled over to the mannequin and started to dress it, sewing the pieces of the outfit together as they worked.

"They've left the magic tape measure on the table," said Kirsty. "Now's our chance to grab it!"

The three fairies edged closer to the golden tape measure, being careful to stay close to the piles of fabric in case they needed to hide quickly. The goblins finished putting the outfit together and stepped back to admire it.

"It's a work of art!" said the skinny goblin.

"Jack Frost will love it," declared the long-nosed goblin.

"They're not looking!" whispered Tyra. "Now's our chance!"

Kirsty reached out her hand and touched the edge of the tape measure. She started to pull it towards her, but just then the long-nosed goblin gave a loud squawk.

"My turn to carry the tape measure now!" he said, snatching it up. "You lot have been hogging it all day."

"No way!" shouted the goblin in the top hat. "It's my turn!"

"Mine!" yelled the other two goblins.

The long-nosed goblin stuck out his tongue at them and then raced off through the shopping centre.

"Get him!" bellowed the goblin with the scarf-belt.

They all ran after him, and the three fairies joined in the chase, flying close to the high ceiling so that they wouldn't be seen.

The long-nosed goblin was a fast runner, and he led the others around the shopping centre at top speed, not caring who he bumped into along the way.

Their shouts and squeals made everyone stare at them.

"Oh, those naughty goblins!" said Tyra. "They are causing so much trouble!"

Rachel and Kirsty couldn't reply – they needed all their energy to fly as fast as they could!

The rowdy goblins hurtled into *Top*

Hats & Tiaras, where the goblin with the scarf-belt skidded into a long rack of wedding dresses and came out wrapped in ivory silk. The others pointed at him and laughed raucously.

"You naughty children!" cried the shop manager. "Out of here at once! Shoo!"

As the goblins scurried out, Rachel and Kirsty noticed a bride coming out of the shop's fitting room. Tears were welling up in her eyes, and there was a big pink stain all down the front of her dress.

"It's ruined," she was saying. "What am I going to do?"

The girls felt very sorry for her, but there was no time to stop and help. They zoomed after the goblins, who were disappearing into the *Comfy Feet Shoe Shop*. Shoes flew up into the air as the goblins charged through the aisles. Everything was plunged into chaos. Customers were waving shoes and yelling. The shop assistant was clutching his hair and shouting into the phone.

"I'm telling you, there's not a single pair of matching shoes in the entire shop!" he was saying. "I've got hordes of angry customers here."

The girls swooped over his head and chased the goblins into the stockroom at the back of the shop. The goblin in the top hat had been distracted by all the shoes and was busy trying on a purple welly and a green-spotted clog. But the others had disappeared!

Mannequin Mischief

"Look – there's a door at the back of the room," said Kirsty.

"But it's closing!" Tyra cried in alarm. "Quick, girls!"

The three fairies zipped towards the exit, and whisked through with a millimetre to spare. Rachel felt the door brush her wings as it shut tight.

"That was close!" she said.

They found themselves back at the
fountain, on the other side from the
workshop. The three
remaining
goblins were
running
around the
fountain
so fast
that they
looked
like blue
blurs.

"How can
we stop them?"
asked Tyra.

Rachel looked around. Nearby was the
Sweet Scoop Ice Cream Parlour with a
tray of free samples outside.

"I've got an idea," she said. "Tyra, can you use your magic to turn the ice-cream samples blue? If we can distract the goblins, we might be able to get the magic tape measure back."

Tyra nodded and sent a jet of rainbow-coloured sparkles over to the tray. Instantly, the ice creams turned ice blue.

A few seconds later, the goblin with the scarf came speeding over to the tray.

"Ice cream – yummy!" he exclaimed. "It's the same colour as the Ice Blue clothes! I've got to try it!"

The skinny goblin joined him, and soon they were wolfing down the delicious ice cream.

"They're so greedy," said Tyra. "They're going to eat all the free ice cream!"

"But where's the goblin with the tape measure?" asked Rachel.

"Over there!" Kirsty exclaimed, pointing.

Instead of gobbling up the blue ice cream with the others, the long-nosed goblin was scurrying back to the workshop with the magic tape measure to finish Jack's outfit. The fairies sighed in disappointment.

"How are we going to get the magic tape measure back now?" asked Tyra.

Kirsty watched as the goblin added some final stitches to the outfit. He looked very pleased with himself, and that gave her an idea.

"I've got a plan," she said. "Tyra, can you turn us back to human-size again, please? If we flatter the goblin, maybe we can distract him from the tape measure."

The girls hid
behind a giant
flowerpot next
to the fountain,
and Tyra waved
her wand again.
Instantly, the girls
were transformed
back to their normal
size. Tyra tucked herself
under Kirsty's hair, and they walked
over to where the goblin was putting the
finishing touches to the outfit.

"What a wonderful creation!" said
Kirsty in a loud voice.

"Whoever designed this must be super-
talented," said Rachel.

The long-nosed goblin puffed out his
chest.

"That was me," he said proudly.

"Wow, that's impressive," said Rachel. "Is it for you?"

The goblin shook his head.

"That's a shame," said Kirsty. "You're so handsome! It would look totally fabulous on you."

"You're right," said the goblin with a sigh.

"You could always trim it down to fit you," Rachel remarked in a soft voice.

The goblin's hands hesitated over the outfit. Then, excitedly he started to trim it down to his size.

59

"Would you like me to measure it for you?" asked Rachel, holding out her hand and hoping that he would give her the tape measure.

"No, that's mine," the goblin snapped. He held on to it tightly, even when he took the outfit into the fitting room to get changed. As soon as the curtain closed, Rachel turned to Kirsty in alarm.

"What are we going to try now?" she whispered.

"Quick, help me move the mannequin over to the fitting room," said Kirsty.

The Jack Frost mannequin moved easily and quietly on its wheels.

"Tyra, can you make yourself sound like Jack Frost?" asked Kirsty in a low voice. "If the goblin believes the real Jack Frost is here, he might hand over the tape measure."

Tyra waved her wand, but then the fitting room curtain swished open and the goblin came out.

"Too soon!" exclaimed Kirsty.

She gave the mannequin a push, sending it skidding towards the goblin.

"Give the magic tape measure to me, you numbskull," said Tyra in Jack Frost's voice.

The goblin froze, and his eyes nearly popped out of his head. All he could see was Jack Frost speeding towards him.

"Help!" he squeaked.

He threw the magic tape measure into the air and made a run for it. As the mannequin crashed into the fitting room, Tyra caught the magic tape measure in her outstretched hand. It immediately shrank to fairy-size.

"I've got it!" she cheered.

Rachel and Kirsty burst into peals of laughter. She was still talking in Jack Frost's voice!

The girls hurried back to the Design-and-Make Competition workshop. Most of the boys and girls had finished their outfits.

"Five more minutes," Jessica announced.

"Oh no!" cried Rachel. "We're not going to have time to fix our outfits!"

A Surprise Competitor!

"I'm not going to let that happen," said
Tyra, who was hiding underneath Kirsty's
hair. "You would have had time if you
hadn't been helping me, so it's only fair
that I help you now."

She gave her wand a little flick, and the
perfect scarf appeared beside the hem of
Kirsty's dress. Some tubes of fabric paint
appeared beside Rachel's jeans.

Quickly, the girls set to work. They fixed the problems as fast as they could, and Rachel had just painted the final stripe on her rainbow when Jessica clapped her hands together.

"Time's up!" she announced. "Thanks to you all for working so hard. It's time to get ready for the competition!"

"All the other outfits look brilliant," said Kirsty, gazing around.

"Thanks to you," said Tyra. "They would have been fashion disasters if you hadn't helped me to get my tape measure back. How can I ever thank you enough?"

"You already have," said Rachel, patting her jeans. "It's been fun!"

"I have to take the tape measure back to Fairyland now," said Tyra. "Goodbye,

Rachel and Kirsty —
and good luck in the
competition!"

She zoomed high
above the fountain, gave
the girls a final wave and
then disappeared in a puff of
rainbow-coloured fairy dust.

The shopping centre was
getting very busy. Lots of people
were arriving to watch the competition.
They gathered around the fountain
as everyone changed into their new
fashions. Kirsty's brightly coloured dress
swirled around her ankles, and the paint
on Rachel's jeans sparkled in the lights.
They felt very proud of their hard work.

"Look, there's your mum in the crowd,"
said Kirsty.

They waved to Mrs Walker and her friend Moira, who was standing beside her. A platform had been built beside the fountain, and all the entrants walked onto it and stood in a row. Rachel and Kirsty squeezed each other's hands.

Jessica and Ella walked onto the stage with a short man in a dark-grey suit.

"Ladies and gentlemen, boys and girls, welcome to the competition," said Jessica with a beaming smile. "The entrants have

been working hard on
their designs, and
now it's our job to
choose the ones
that will take part
in the fashion
show."

Now Ella
stepped forward.

"Jessica and I
will be judging the
competition, together with the manager
of *Hartley's Department Store*, Owen
Jacobs. Please be patient while we make
our decisions."

The three judges started to walk along
the line. They examined each design
closely and carefully. But they had only
looked at a couple of entries when there

was a scuffle in the crowd and then a late
entrant ran onto the stage. He had spiky
hair and a nasty scowl.

"It's Jack Frost!" cried Rachel.

The Ice Lord elbowed his way into the
line. He was wearing the outfit that the
goblins had made, but it was much too
small for him. When the judges reached
him, they all exchanged surprised glances.

"Er, well, it's a good effort," said Owen.
"But it's a little on the
small side."

Jack Frost
narrowed his eyes.

"You need
to practise
measuring,"
said Jessica
kindly.

Jack Frost curled his lip.

"Perhaps it might look better on one of your little friends, who we met earlier?" asked Ella.

At this, Jack Frost looked as if steam might come out of his ears!

"You don't know what you're talking about!" he roared. "I'll show you what real fashion means, just you wait and see!"

As he turned and stormed off the platform, there was a loud ripping sound and a split tore up the back of his trousers.

"I wonder what he meant by that," said Kirsty quietly.

But there was no time for Rachel to reply. The judges had reached them! The girls held their breath as Jessica, Ella and Owen walked around them, looking at their outfits.

"These are great outfits," said Owen. "I especially like the creative flair of the scarf-dress!"

"The detail in your rainbow is wonderful," Ella told Rachel with a smile.

"We'd love you to model your outfits in the fashion show at the end of the week," said Jessica. "Well done, both of you!"

The girls were thrilled, and they gave each other a big hug. In the crowd, Mrs Walker was smiling and clapping.

"I'm so excited!" whispered Rachel, as the judges moved on. "I just hope that we can stop Jack Frost before the fashion show. There are still four magical objects to find."

"Of course we can," said Kirsty firmly. "The fairies are depending on us, and we're not going to let them down!"

**Now it's time for Kirsty and
Rachel to help...**

Alexa the Fashion Reporter Fairy

Read on for a sneak peek...

"What shall we call our fashion
magazine, Rachel?" Kirsty asked, tapping
her pencil thoughtfully on her sketch pad.
"I just can't think of a good title!"

The girls were in the beautiful
landscaped park that surrounded the
new *Tippington Fountains Shopping
Centre*, an enormous building of chrome
and glass. Kirsty had come to stay with
Rachel for half-term, and Mrs Walker
had taken them to the grand opening
of *Tippington Fountains* earlier that
week. Yesterday Rachel and Kirsty had
attended a workshop for the Design-

and-Make Competition at the shopping centre, and the girls had enjoyed it so much, they'd decided to create their own fashion magazine. They were sitting on a picnic rug on a soft carpet of red, yellow and orange autumn leaves with their pads and coloured pencils.

Rachel was finishing a design for a T-shirt. "I'm not sure," she replied, glancing up as more leaves drifted down from the trees above them. "*Fashion for Girls*?"

"How about *Fantastic Fashions*?" suggested Rachel's dad. He was sitting nearby on a park bench, reading a newspaper.

"*Fabulous Fashions*?" Kirsty said, then shook her head. "No, that's not special enough. What about *Fashion Magic*?"

"Perfect!" Rachel said with a grin. She

held up her sketch pad to show Kirsty her T-shirt design. The T-shirt was bright orange with "Tippington Fountains" written in gold and red letters across the front. Below the words Rachel had added a drawing of the spectacular fountains that were situated in the middle of the shopping centre.

Read Alexa the Fashion Reporter Fairy to find out what adventures are in store for Kirsty and Rachel!

Meet the
Fashion Fairies

If Kirsty and Rachel don't find the Fashion Fairies'
magical objects, Jack Frost will ruin fashion forever!

www.rainbowmagicbooks.co.uk

Meet the fairies, play games
and get sneak peeks at
the latest books!

www.rainbowmagicbooks.co.uk

There's fairy fun for everyone on
our wonderful website.
You'll find great activities, competitions, stories and
fairy profiles, and also a special newsletter.

Get 30% off all Rainbow Magic books at
www.rainbowmagicbooks.co.uk

Enter the code RAINBOW at the checkout.
Offer ends 31 December 2012.

Offer valid in United Kingdom and Republic of Ireland only.

Competition!

Here's a friend who Kirsty and Rachel met in an earlier story. Use the clues below to help you guess her name. When you have enjoyed all seven of the Fashion Fairies books, arrange the first letters of each mystery fairy's name to make a special word, then send us the answer!

CLUES

1. This fairy wears a necklace with a star on it.

2. She is one of the Ocean Fairies.

3. This fairy has a sea creature friend called Spike.

The fairy's name is _ _ _ _ _ _ _ _ _ the _ _ _ _ _ _ _ Fairy

We will put all of the correct entries into a draw and select one winner to receive a special Fashion Fairies goody bag. Your name will also be featured in a forthcoming Rainbow Magic story!

Enter online now at www.rainbowmagicbooks.co.uk

The Complete Book of Fairies

Packed with secret fairy facts
and extra-special rainbow reveals, this magical guide
includes all you need to know about your favourite
Rainbow Magic friends.

Out Now!